ONE
TO THREE

RAMONA SAPPHIRE

authorHOUSE®

AuthorHouse™
1663 Liberty Drive
Bloomington, IN 47403
www.authorhouse.com
Phone: 1 (800) 839-8640

Ameedah Mawalin
1507 East 53rd Street, Suite 314
Chicago, Illinois 60615
(773) 981-7409
amawaln@yahoo.com
www.sapphirewithpassion.com

Published by AuthorHouse 01/10/2017

ISBN: 978-1-5246-5806-9 (sc)
ISBN: 978-1-5246-5805-2 (e)

Print information available on the last page.

This book is printed on acid-free paper.

Author's Note

Thanks so much for selecting my publication for your reading pleasure. I enjoy writing stories on assorted topics based on experience and overall -- imagination. I'll admit I'm a bit eccentric and quirky. Many of my stories may comprise an element of inspiration, are outrageous, raunchy, mysterious, bizarre, insightful, or even simple, to say the least. And most recently, cringe humor and spoof writing has been added to my repertoire of genres.

A very special thanks to those who believed in me, inspired, pushed, and supported me, and appreciated my own distinct style of story-telling rather comparing me to others.

Very special thanks to the well-meaning critics that compelled the necessary *expedient* changes. Your expertise has been far-reaching and helpful, for which I am eternally grateful.

Foremost, are my thanks to God via the gift of breath and hence the wit, imagination, strength, and courage to inspire others and to keep dreaming and pushing.

And lastly, thanks to my mother for her unconditional support and belief in me.

Prologue

Tyrell had all kinda crazy going on. He was a normal red-blooded guy with laudable ambitions and needs. Formerly, he'd had women galore revolving around him like a turnstile. He reckoned he could simply keep playing the field and have his way despite the repercussions and consequences. And that'd worked for a hot minute until he'd narrowed it down to three. That's when he'd decided to choose and settle down.

It all started under a full moon and crisp starry night when the four strangers were among the massive cruisers aboard the same midnight pajama party boat, the Naughtycal King and Queen Cruiseliner, this past Summer. Tyrell, a charismatic savvy mechanic, had taken this opportunity to hustle with flyers about his services.

Ashley and Regina, a couple of harebrained avid bus riders, mind you, thirstily phoned Tyrell the following afternoon. Months later, Tamara, rather straight-laced, needed an oil change and Tyrell was running a special. And the games began…

Chapter 1

"You said you were going to call me. I've been waiting all day. Did you forget about me?" asked Ashley, twentyish, average height, with a mid-back weave.

Tyrell, thirtyish, lanky, and average-looking was nuzzling Regina's ear on the sofa in his one-bedroom man cave when Ashley's text came through. He sneak-peeked it on his cell phone and ignored it.

"Aren't you going to answer that? That buzzing's driving me crazy," said twenty-something Regina, full-lipped, thick, and buxom, with a horsetail-weave ponytail.

"It's nobody. It's just a friend who needs to borrow money and I can't help him right now."

"Uhn-hun."

"So where were we?" asked Tyrell.

Later on that evening, Tyrell returned Ashley's text and begged her to come over. She responded with a phone call.

"You think I want to be with you after you shamed me like that?"

"Please, baby, please! I had a lot of stuff to do and my boy needed some ends from me. I had to track him down and he held me up."

"Uhn-hun. Well since you returned my texts, I suppose I can swing by."

"Hey, can you stop and get us some beer? I didn't get a chance to get any with all the running around I was doing and all."

"You know, you always seem to be out of beer every time I come over. What's up with that?"

"Because my boy always takes a big chunk of my ends. Sometimes I think he's on somethin.' I'll tell you what, to make it up to you, I'll cook you a nice dinner. How's that?"

"Really?"

"Yes baby, I promise. So guestimate when you think you're going to make it here so I can know when to have it ready."

"Oh, in about an hour or so."

"Perfecto Mondo!"

Tyrell snagged the top ramen, canned beans, and canned vegetables of carrots, peas, pearl onions, and mushrooms from the kitchen cabinet and whipped up a meal. Tyrell was in his boxers when Ashley appeared at the door from the bus with the liquor all dolled up and amazing-looking. She'd anticipated fireworks--a romantic dinner with candlelight and all the trimmings. Tyrell answered the door.

"What happened? Where's your pants? Did I catch you at a bad time?" asked Ashley, stumped by Tyrell's attire, posing outside the door with the liquor and attempting to sneak peek inside.

"My bad. I spilled some crap on my pants when I was cooking. Hey, can you help a brotha out and wash them out for me? They're in the bedroom." It'd never occurred to Ashley that Tyrell could've simply changed into another pair, so rooted in dingbatism.

"Oh, alright. I suppose I can do that. Here, take this bag," said Ashley, shoving it at him.

Tyrell placed the beers in the fridge. He danced a little jig. He was ecstatic. "Looks like I'mma get me some before dinner," he rejoiced. "She fell smackdab for the okey doke so now all's I've got to do is mix everything together and stick it in the microwave later," he mumbled. Next, he slithered to the bedroom with a Cheshire Cat smile.

After their fully dressed quickie, mind you, Tyrell freshened up and emerged from the bedroom while Ashley was in the bedroom's adjoining bathroom. Ashley lingered behind to tidy herself up, redo her makeup, and spruce up her hairdo unaware of Tyrell's lack of wardrobe change. Besides, she was too preoccupied with expecting him to have candles lit and the meal placed on the table with all the trimmings of a romantic dinner. Really? Didn't she know him by now after two weeks of this cat and mouse crap?

Ashley waivered a while longer to enable Tyrell to get it all together. She was ecstatic. What happened to his so-called soiled trousers was anybody's guess. Apparently, Ashley had forgotten about them.

Tyrell, boxers and all, was at the table dishing his goo from the microwave onto paper plates with plastic utensils and paper napkins when Ashley emerged from the bedroom. No table setting, no candles, nada!

Ashley paused in disbelief and indignation. She would've left, too, had she not been so ravished and ready to gnaw her foot off. She'd spent her last dime on the beer.

Dammit to hell!

Chapter 2

Tyrell and Tamara enjoyed a candlelight dinner at a modest restaurant. Tamara, a degreed, medium-built, hour-glass-shaped, loosely twisted-haired, bling-bling/animal/classical print-wearing, Buppy brunette wasn't that particular as long she was treated respectfully. She was all about a man doing what was within his means rather fronting. He'd pulled out her chair when she arrived and everything. Life was good.

The restaurant hosted a band and was cozy and quaint. "May I have this dance?" Tyrell posed to Tamara. She proffered her hand and they glided together on the dance floor. They engaged in a little stepping and the couple appeared to be connecting and enjoying themselves.

The couple returned to the table and dined and chit-chatted. When the bill arrived, Tamara excused herself immediately; she knew the drill. Now that was a first, thought Tyrell. Usually *he* was the first one to bolt.

Tamara purposefully took an extraordinary amount of time, ensuring Tyrell paid the bill out of sheer awkwardness, no doubt. She gazed at her image pleasingly in the full-length mirror. She wore an animal-print formfitting dress, with sheer hose, spike-heeled red pumps, and white pearl accessories. She puckered her lips, painted them scarlet red, and winked at herself. "How you like me now?" she whispered pompously.

Right on the money, as planned, the bill folder was indeed gone upon Tamara's return and Tyrell was nursing the last of his coffee. He was irritated as hell.

"What's wrong?" asked Tamara.

"You took a little long," said Tyrell.

"Well a girl needs her time to make herself pretty. You don't think I wake up like this, do you?"

Scary troll dolls and witches crossed Tyrell's mind. "Well, I'm ready to go," he said. "What say you?"

"I'm ready when you are."

They both stood and Tyrell proceeded ahead of Tamara who didn't budge. He'd made it all the way to his vehicle parked at the curbside before realizing she wasn't beside him. He swiveled toward the restaurant and glared through the large picture window. Tamara was merely standing frozen at her seat eyeballing him with a half-ass smile.

Tyrell sprinted through the door and said, "I'm so sorry. Excuse my manners. Here, let me assist you with your wrap."

Tamara smiled and said sweetly, "Thank you."

Tyrell placed it gingerly around Tamara's shoulders with her assistance and ushered her to his vehicle. He was about to hop into the driver's side when he remembered to open the door for her. He assisted her into the passenger side and climbed into the driver's side and took off.

Beneath a rustic clear sky, tarrying along, the stuffed travelers listened to the radio and karaoked together. No bitching, no whining? Say what? Tyrell was impressed. He was truly having an amazing time and digging on Tamara. She asked Tyrell about himself, appearing to be genuinely interested--appearing being the operative word.

Tyrell traveled the road to Franklinton, *The Bottoms*, an up and coming gentrified area of the inner city of Columbus, Ohio. It was formerly declared a floodplain until a floodwall was built as a barricade against the flooding.

Tyrell arrived at Tamara's residence and remembered to come to the passenger side and assist her out his vehicle. He escorted her to her door.

"Tyrell, I had an amazing time; it was fun. Call me if you feel like it, and if not, it's been real," she said coyly.

What? I've never heard this stuff before, thought Tyrell. Contrarily, Ashley and Regina would've sweated me. Hhm, she's kind of tough, but sweet; an undercover kind of crazy perhaps, but doable, he thought. I wonder what would happen if I tried to kiss her. Well, I won't know until I try—right? Oh, what the hell, he thought. So he leaned in.

Tamara responded tenderly with closed lips. She didn't mind a kiss to show she was interested, but no tongue on the first date; not on my watch, she thought. They disengaged and Tamara hesitated. I know he doesn't think I'm going to invite his ass in. He better get on away from here, ole rascal, she chuckled to herself.

I might as well leave, thought Tyrell. I don't think she's the type of gal who would do a guy on the first date.

Tamara decided to help him out instead of keeping him in a quandary and guessing. "Good night," she said.

"Good night," Tyrell responded. "I'll call you."

"Hey, it's okay with me if you do or don't. But I'll be looking forward to hearing from you if you decide to." And she turned and disappeared inside.

"Really?" he mumbled. I'm definitely going to call her, he thought. She's not like the others. She likes to move slowly and I likes that in her. And he returned to his car, eyeballed her door once more, and pulled off.

Chapter 3

Tyrell and his buddies, Gunner and Luke, dressed in silk pajamas, crossed the gangway into the small atrium of the Naughtycal King and Queen Cruiseliner. Their eyes feasted on a bar, piano, DJ stage, which was vacant for now, and a sweeping staircase leading to the party decks. The scenery was breathtaking on the upscale mini cruiseliner. The sunset was like a strobe light against the skyline and the city lights were glistening. Passengers are led under historic bridges to a view of Downtown Cleveland's skyline along the lake and riverfront. There were minimally three decks of boom box DJ music, unlimited buffets, luscious desserts, coffee and tea, and cash bars.

The threesome scrambled to the bar to nab their cocktails before the lines became ridiculously long. With shrimp cocktails in hand, they leaned against the deck railing to gaze down upon the passengers flowing from the gangway to the atrium. Their eyes beheld, among a dollop of men here and there, a sea of booty and weave that mesmerized them. Anything and everything was fair game among this adults-only soiree from negligees, to corsets, nighties, baby dolls, camisole tops and shorts, peignoir sets, garter belts, and peek-a-boos. They were ecstatic.

"Man, there's gonna be a whole lot of jingling up in here and it ain't even Christmas," said Gunner. And Tyrell and Luke cracked up.

The remainder of the guests poured into the atrium and scrambled to miscellaneous decks like ants. The ship pulled off and the cruise officially began. Within forty-five minutes the music was thumping fiercely and the passengers and the boat rocking.

Several couples and groups corralled on the observation decks to sneak away for a romantic embrace or simply to enjoy the breathtaking view of the glimmering skyline and downtown attractions.

Tamara donned in a leopard swing dress and fur-trimmed stiletto slip-ons and shawl, was among the passengers on the climate-controlled observation desk. She'd managed to find a secluded spot. Tyrell making his rounds passing out his flyers regarding his services as a mechanic at the auto shop he was employed at eyed Tamara's backside admiringly. He decided to approach her and slid beside her.

"Excuse, me, hello, my name's Tyrell."

"Well, hello, pleased to meet you. Mine is Tamara. Whatchu got there?" asked Tamara eyeing the flyers.

"Oh these little ole things. It's nothing. Just some flyers about my business. I'm a mechanic and I work at an auto shop and was just passing these out about my services."

"Impressive. I love men who work with their hands like that. Are you good at it?"

"The best. In fact, I'm considering having my own shop soon, once I find some good investors. And if you want to see how good I am for yourself, check me out." And he handed Tamara a flyer.

"Oh, you're in Columbus, that's good. Because I was going to tell you I don't live in Cincinnati. This party sounded like so much fun when they advertised it on the radio."

"For real. And so far I'm having a great time, especially now that I've met you, except for these two thirsty sistahs that keep kinda stalking me. My buddies have been trying to get at'em too but apparently they're not attracted to them, so they're after me. So what do you do?"

"Well I..."

"Tyrell! Finally caught up to you. Where you been hiding? I've been looking for you over the past half hour. These two creeps keep stalking me and my friend, Regina," said Ashley, whose perky breasts and pointy nipples were fully outlined through her nightie.

Your friend? thought Tyrell, uncontrollably ogling Ashley under Tamara's discerning eye. Didn't she know her friend was stalking him too? Well, he sure wasn't about to be the one to break the news to her.

Ashley pulled Tyrell by the hand and said, "Let's dance!" with Tyrell reluctantly allowing himself to be pulled away and Tamara cracking up and shaking her head sympathetically at him.

Tyrell's buddies finally caught up to him all sweaty from dancing their butts off, and Regina, Ashley's friend, had caught up to her. It turns out Tamara got lost in the shuffle with this looser guy with thermal pajamas on who'd apparently forgotten his jock strap. He was grinding on her, and though she had to keep pushing him away, she allowed him to have his fun. At times she was having fun herself with his goofy ass too, though his rhythm sucked and he had a bit of nystagmus.

Ashley and Regina, dressed in gossamer nighties with matching panties and gowns, were fiercely duking it out for the attention of Tyrell, attempting to out-dance each other with the sleaziest moves they could muster. Gunner and Luke likewise were competing for the attention of Ashley and Regina making buffoons of themselves.

When the boat turned around and headed back to the docks at the end of the night, Tyrell frantically searched for Tamara who was nowhere to be found. Ashley and Regina had made it back to the atrium and were scrambling down the gangway. They spotted Tyrell and each surreptitiously eyed him and motioned with their lips, "I'll call you," neither one of them owning a vehicle. Simultaneously, Gunner and Luke spotted them and waved good bye and pitched them the 'I'll-call-you' lip sync and telephone hand motion.

Ashley was the first one to respond to the flyer. She'd boarded a bus and arrived at Tyrell's door the following afternoon. She was like the Sahara Desert. Talking about thirsty!

Chapter 4

Tyrell retired to bed feeling rather mellow that night. He'd never met anyone like Tamara before. All his other ladies were *sweating him!*

This one was reserved; perhaps a little too reserved for his taste, however, he was open for the adventure. On second thought, perhaps she's an undercover nutcase. A twirling-head, lacerated-faced, psychotic Voodoo doll came to mind. Tyrell decided to play it cool and avoid calling her right away to ascertain if she was legit.

Tyrell waited, and waited, and waited, and three days lapsed. Within those measly three days, Ashley and Regina must've called and texted him umpteen times. They were sweating him like a sauna.

In the interim, Tyrell lured them to his place and continued to pull off the same shenanigans of juggling them yet convincing them they each were his one and only, which wasn't exactly a bad thing. I mean what girl doesn't want to feel special--right? he thought.

It was a shame Tyrell had to play such games versus being authentic. Women were so naïve, he thought. After all, he was single, playing the field, and struggling to make a decision. Didn't they know this? Seemingly, it was up to them to keep their legs closed and not become attached, which was the one thing that set Tamara apart from the others. She'd kept him an honest man so far, so he imagined. Later on...

"I know she's over there!" accused Regina. "Look, I'm not putting up with this nonsense. I'mma leave your sorry ass!"

"Who are you talking about? There's nobody here," said Tyrell.

"Look, you gotta go!" insisted Tyrell, abruptly, turning to Ashley beside him on his sofa.

"Why? I just got here about two hours ago."

"And your point is…"

"I planned to stay the night."

Look, the fellas are coming over any minute to play cards and you're not welcomed."

"Why?"

"Because it's my guy time. No women allowed."

Ashley, disgruntled, pouted and pulled up her panties and lowered her dress.

"Holla when you're ready. I'm just going to the bedroom to make a quick call."

"You're calling her, aren't you?"

"Why do you keep sweating me? You know you're my one and only. And he seized her about the waist, planted her with a mushy kiss, and headed for the bedroom.

Tyrell dialed Tamara's number for the second time. Again, the poor slob hung up without as much as leaving a message. He returned to the living room to send Ashley off, frustrated than a mug.

"See you tomorrow, baby?"

"Sure." And they kissed one last time and she departed for the bus.

In the next instant, Tyrell responded to Regina's last text wherein she was threatening to cut him off, saying, "Suit yourself." Contrarily, within the next hour or so, she'd bussed it over to his place and they'd gotten busy.

Afterwards, Tyrell propped himself against his headboard foregoing his usual after-sex kiss. He tumbled out of bed, donned his boxers, and seized his cell phone. He was preoccupied with Tamara now and the fact that she hadn't called or texted him yet. This threw him for a loop.

"Where are you going so fast and why are you taking your cell phone?" asked Regina.

"To be a grown-ass man and mind my own damn business!" And Regina, disgruntled, rolled her eyes and hurled a pillow at Tyrell's head.

Tyrell shut the bedroom door behind himself and disappeared into the living room. He dialed Tamara's number and received no answer;

he was too delusional to leave a message. He returned to the bedroom to find Regina fully dressed.

"Where are you going?"

"Look, I meant it! I'm not putting up with this mess! I don't know why I bothered to come over here anyway!"

By now Tyrell had returned his focus to Regina and was hot for her. "Probably because of this," he said, dropping his boxers, stiff as a pole. Needless to say, the pair romped and sexed each other throughout the remainder of the night.

Two days later after several repeats of much the same scenario between Ashley and Regina, Tyrell phoned Tamara and finally got a hold of her.

"Hello."

"Hey, this is Tyrell. I've been trying to reach you for a few days."

"Hhm, I didn't receive any message from you."

"I know because I thought you'd recognize the caller ID and call me back."

"Now why'd you think that?"

"Because most women would."

"Now what's my name again?"

"Tamara."

"Good, because I never told you it was Most Women."

"I stand corrected; my bad. So why didn't you call me back again?"

"Because you didn't ask me to."

"Yes I did—oh right. I kept calling and hanging up, didn't I? My bad. And I didn't even have the decency to ask you to call me. I assumed you'd recognize my number and call me back. And before you say anything—I know the old adage; assume means making an ass out of you and me."

"Now that's not what I was going to say at all. I was going to say, I'm very pleased to hear from you and ask you what you've been up to over these past couple of days."

"Oh."

Tamara was training Tyrell who was oblivious to this. She'd learned to show instead of tell a man how she desired to be treated.

Bitching and moaning wasn't her style, nor was she trying to bully him. She'd listened to his troubles and sympathized, however felt no compunction whatsoever to aid and abet him; that was strictly reserved for a committed relationship with an engagement and a wedding date. She'd learned how to pamper her man without sheltering him and turning him into a wuss.

"Would you like to go out again?"

"Sure," said Tamara.

"Where to?"

"You name the time and place," she said encouragingly.

Tamara continued to amaze Tyrell. His other ladies would've chosen a fancy-schmancy place that'd bust open his wallet. Then they'd bitch and moan when he'd dodge the pricier stuff on the menu.

Tyrell desired to impress this lady. She was laid back, classy, and easy on the eyes and wallet, and quite a listener and a potential partner who would have his back and support his dreams as his lady, so he imagined. She was the one he wanted to commit to for the long haul so far.

Chapter 5

"How about I pick you up tonight about seven and we catch a movie?" asked Tyrell.

"Great; sounds like a plan."

"What type of movies do you like?"

"Mostly romantic comedies and action pictures—not too violent though."

"Gotcha."

There was an awkward pause. Tamara believed in letting a man lead the conversation for the most part. "Okay, see you then," said Tyrell, breaking the silence.

"See you then," responded Tamara, who promptly hung up.

Tyrell lingered on the phone and thought, I can't wait until we get past this awkward stage and finally get busy. Perhaps she'll allow me to feel her up a bit in the show.

The pair arrived at the AMC Lennox Town Center 24 Theater on Kinnear Road and Tamara was surprisingly accommodating and endearing toward Tyrell. After all, it's not like she wasn't attracted to him, and there was no harm in a little petting and kissing, right? And to add icing to the cake, she'd worn a skirt! He was blown away and ecstatic.

Tyrell and Tamara paused at the concession counter for popcorn and sodas to share. They headed for their seats. Tamara allowed Tyrell to select the seating as she eagerly followed. Midway into the flick, Tyrell made his first move.

Timidly, Tyrell placed one hand on Tamara's knee and massaged it gingerly. Tamara surprisingly covered his hand and turned to him and cheesed. Okay, that went rather well, he thought. Now let's see here, next move, hand on lap. Tamara cheesed again. Okay, so far, so good. Now let's try a kiss. Tamara was fully open to it. Ok, here comes the tongue. Tamara was receptive and reciprocated.

Now, this last one is going to be tricky, thought Tyrell. He was a bit jittery and edgy. His hands were clammy and shaky.

Tyrell abruptly envisioned himself yesterday at least three rows down, his head shoved into a seat, with his legs dangling upwards, and his taste buds scampering about the floor like marbles behind his next move. Yeah, Tamara had it like that alright, so he imagined. She'd slap him into yesterday and the taste out his mouth. He knew better than to push her buttons. Despite this, he decided to throw caution to the wind and give it a shot anyway.

Okay, I'mma go for gold now, thought Tyrell. Eagerly, he eased his hand up Tamara's skirt to her thigh. Tamara received it warmly, squirming and cheesing. The couple kissed passionately. Triumphant theme music played in Tyrell's head. And just as he made a beeline for her panties, a firm grip stopped him! Tyrell, crestfallen, swiftly withdrew his hand. Okay, so much for that, but hey, it was worth a shot, he thought. He sneak-peeked Tamara's expression to ascertain her reaction, who eyed him coolly.

Later, the pair swung by Rally's to get a couple of burgers, fries, and sodas. They chatted, giggled, and shared stories.

Tyrell's phone had been buzzing off the hook throughout the evening. Normally, if he was with Ashley or Regina when this occurred, they'd blow up at him and cuss him out, or attempt to lay a guilt-trip on him to shame him.

However, they'd manifested to Tyrell they weren't going anywhere despite their humiliation. Clearly, they didn't value themselves or him either for that matter. They'd presumed their abrasiveness was putting him in his place, hence making them appear confident, when in fact Tyrell perceived them otherwise.

Tyrell performed his usual chivalry of opening and closing doors for Tamara. Just as he pulled up to her apartment, he turned to her.

"So where do you see this relationship going?"

"So far, so good. I'm having a great time and I feel good about it."

"That's great to hear because I'm digging you too. I'm considering giving up playing the field and just dating *you*," said Tyrell, albeit his cell phone buzzing off the hook that very moment, which was preceded by a deluge of texts and calls earlier.

"Why? That won't be necessary. We can just take it slow and keep kicking it. Neither of us has a ring on our finger, so there's no rush," concluded Tamara emphatically.

Now while this was all new and refreshing to Tyrell, he truly desired to get to know Tamara without the interference of other women swimming around in his head. "Yeah, but I want to know that you're only seeing me and I, you. I totally want to connect with you and for us to be exclusive."

"Let's just keep seeing each other a little while longer and we'll see. It's really sweet of you though to want to be committed. It's not every day that a gal hears those words. I'm truly flattered," said Tamara.

Flattered? Did she just say flattered? Where in the hell did she come from--Mars? Yet her defensiveness was provoking his interest further. She's not sweating me like the others, and it's turning me on, he thought. She's warm, friendly, and caring. And I know she's digging on me because of all the liberties she allowed at the show tonight despite the last part. What more can a man ask for? Tyrell thought.

Perhaps we can have a business together or something. I wonder if she's a good cook. Pretty soon, she'll be propositioning me to come over or I'll ask her to my place when the time's right, supposed Tyrell.

Once home, Tamara lingered in her seat for Tyrell to arrive to the passenger side and open the door. She proffered her hand and he assisted her out his vehicle. He escorted her to her door and kissed and squeezed her goodnight. She was fully receptive to him and gave him a little play.

Tamara could feel his stiffening against her as he squeezed her rather tightly and leaned in as far as he could. That was her cue to disengage from him.

"Aren't you going to let me in? asked Tyrell, with bedroom eyes.

"Not yet." And she turned and unlocked the door and slipped through it.

Tyrell beamed at the door momentarily, wallowing in Tamara's touch and perfume. He cast a Cheshire Cat smile. "It's coming," he said coyly, and sprinted to his vehicle and departed.

Chapter 6

Over the next couple of weeks, Tyrell and Tamara dated on the regular. They were truly hitting it off. Tyrell was wining and dining her so tough, he was wearing a hole in his wallet. He'd relayed to Tamara all his business goals and his desire for a partner.

Tamara would support Tyrell by listening intently and lovingly, asking questions of concern, and acknowledging his dreams and plans. However, she offered nothing beyond that, although she envisioned real potential in him. He was alluding to the two of them being partners. He was attempting to wear her down. If only he knew.

Meanwhile, there was boatloads of drama transpiring between himself, Ashley, and Regina. Both had refused to let go despite Tyrell's pleas. He'd refrained from telling either of them he was in a committed relationship due to fear of the repercussions and consequences.

He'd envisioned their retaliation via his spray-painted vehicle and the entrance to his place and what not. And furthermore envisioned wombats circling him and Ghoulies. He was out of sorts with worry and anticipation.

Tyrell was right about one thing; they sweated him indeed and sent him hurtful angry texts. They banged on his door at all times of the night and texted nonstop. However, he stuck to his guns and failed to respond. And when he didn't hear from them after two weeks, he kicked up his heels and chanted the Martin Luther King "Free at last..." mantra.

Feeling wholly exonerated, Tyrell decided to pop up at Tamara's place unannounced. He had flowers and candy handy. He was smelling delicious and dressed to the nines. He knocked boldly on her door.

Tamara stared through her peep hole and cracked the door. "What are you doing here?" she asked perplexed, yet pleased.

"I thought I'd surprise you and come see you, seeing how you're my girl and all."

"Your girl? We're just kicking it--remember?"

"Yes, I know, but I've decided to cut all my dates loose and now there's just you. You like me don't you?"

"Sure, you're quite sweet and fun to be with and all, but…"

"But what? Are you telling me you've changed your mind?"

"Changed my mind about what?"

"Going together."

"I never agreed to that. I said we needed to stay connected and then see what happens next, to paraphrase."

"Well, I think we're at NEXT. So what say you we call it a commitment?"

"Hey babe, your meal is getting cold," announced a baritone from inside.

"Who's that?! Your brother?!"

"No."

"Father?!"

"No."

"Cousin?!"

"No."

"Transgender sister?!"

"No, for the last time, and none of your business. And I told you I live alone—you know that."

"Then who's that?!"

"Again, none of your business," Tamara replied softly, sympathizing with Tyrell's concern.

"Wait, are you on a date?"

"Maybe—maybe not."

"Babe, come on!" squawked the baritone.

"Look I've got to go! Thank you for the candy and the beautiful flowers. We'll talk later, okay?" And Tamara shut the door in Tyrell's face softly.

"Oh no she didn't!" said Tyrell, animated. "We'll just have to see about that. So long sweetheart!" And he stormed to his car and sped off.

Tamara's phone was jumping off the hook that night. "Who is that calling you like that, babe?" asked Dexter, her hunky date and lover.

"Oh just a good friend. Look, I'll just put this thing away so we won't be disturbed." And the two of them got busy.

Tamara was wise enough to know that playing the field was a woman's prerogative just like a man's, except sex was an option rather a must for a woman. By choice, Hunky Dexter was serving as her layover booty-call man to perhaps guard her vulnerability and for restraint until she found her husband. He was down for the cause and drama-free, with no strings attached, so she imagined. They were careful and used protection.

Tamara wasn't into double-dipping when it came to sex; she believed in one chip at a time. Besides, she had her friends, family, and career.

Chapter 7

Tyrell fraught with insecurity tossed and turned that night. He judged he was being played. He wondered if pursuing Tamara was worth his while. In the next instant he concluded, hell yeah! He was down for the chase. She was polished, well-bred, and a successful health insurance claims adjuster. He could see a future with her. Most of all, she was drama-free, so he imagined, and had the right to play the field too, "uh I guess," he reasoned aloud.

"I'm just going to have to step up my game," Tyrell mumbled to himself over a cup of coffee the following morning. "First thing I'm going to do is back off her for a few days and stop sweating her—Yeah, that's how I'm going play it. And if she feels any kind of way about me, she'll call. Yeah, after three whole days, she'll be thirsty for somma Tyrell," he mumbled.

By the end of each night, Tyrell waxed and waned in his bed and stared at his cell phone. Okay, okay, he reasoned. She's probably busy right now. She'll call me perhaps tomorrow. DAY TWO: Same scenario—no phone call. DAY THREE: 8:00 a.m., 12:00 p.m., 4:00 p.m., 8:00 p.m.—and still no phone call.

At eight o'clock that evening, Tyrell, frustrated, decided to take a nap for two hours. His usual bedtime was around ten o'clock. The alarm clock sounded and he stretched. And still laying supine, he stared at his cell phone waiting for it to ring until his eyelids collapsed and he crashed.

You know what, I'm just going to have to drop my pride and call Tamara and see what happens. If she doesn't respond, then I know I'm wasting my time, Tyrell thought over a cup of coffee at his kitchen table the following morning. Hhm, back where I started from I see.

Tamara's phone rang three times and Tyrell was about to give up when a panting voice responded.

"Hello?"

"Oh, you answered. I'm surprised. I thought you forgot about me."

"And why'd you think that?"

"Because I haven't heard from you."

"And neither have I from you."

"Oh well, seeing how you had company and all, I thought, uh, you would be tied up and get back to me when you were free."

Momentarily, Tamara envisioned Hunky Dexter banging her with her wrists tied to her bedposts. "Well, actually I thought I ran *you* away, seeing how annoyed you were."

"So then why didn't you call?"

"Because I allow the dog to chase the cat. I'm assertive, but not aggressive. That's not my style. So next time you want to hear from me, just give me a jingle, okay?"

"Gotcha. So what's cooking? I've been wining and dining you on the regular. My money's a little funny. So how about you treat me to dinner this time?"

"Sure, sounds fair. I'll invite you to my place. I think I can trust you a bit now. So how does seven sound?"

"Great!"

"Okay, see you at seven, my place. Bye."

"Bye."

Chapter 8

Tamara searched in her kitchen cabinet and pulled out a couple of cans of baked beans. Peering in her refrigerator, she pulled out a package of turkey franks, placed them in a skillet, added a bottle of spaghetti sauce, and whipped them together. "Uhm," tasty she said. "Now alls I gotta do is let this here cool, put it in the fridge, and take it and heat it in the microwave when Tyrell comes. Let's see what I can serve with this; oh yeah some Kool-Aid with these here little packets, and some toast, and some of these here little pudding packs from my niece's lunch pack. Oh, and these here crackers I saved from all the soup and salad from this week. Now let me see if I have any paper plates, napkins, and plastic dinnerware. Oh goody, just enough here. Okay, last but not least, let me have these here tea lights handy. This will help to set the mood," she concluded to herself and chuckled.

Tyrell arrived promptly at seven that evening with a bottle of wine. He'd planned to use it to loosen Tamara up with the hopes of getting lucky tonight, so he imagined. He anticipated a steak dinner and the works on her fine china, candle lights, fancy napkins, and a bangin' dessert. He was hyped.

"Come on in," said Tamara, ushering him through. He was stumped. The apartment was a studio. He could've sworn it was roomier from the looks of it on the outside. Is she who she purports to be or was she just fronting? he thought.

The lights were so bright they stabbed his eyes. Tyrell was expecting Tamara to be in sexy attire like she dresses for him on dates. Contrarily, she was dressed in a granny grumps, knee-length, over-sized, floral-patterned moo-moo with her furry slippers on. A silver-haired, snaggletooth granny with pendulant waist-length boobs came to mind as he eyed her.

"You look nice," said Tamara, cheesing at him. Too bad I can't say the same about you, Tyrell thought, cheesing back.

"So you didn't say how I look," said Tamara, putting him on blast.

"Uh, you look nice and comfy. I like that pattern." He *HATED* it!

"Why thanks. So there's the restroom to your left and I'll take your jacket. And by the time you return, I'll have dinner on the table. You hungry?"

"Sure. And here's a bottle of wine."

"You didn't have to do that," said Tamara, seizing it from him. "How thoughtful of you."

"Yeah, that's me, Mr. Thoughtful alright. I'll see you in a minute."

"Sure, everything will be ready."

Tyrell was curious. He smelled something, alright, he thought, but it didn't' seem like it was coming from the oven. She'd recently told him she hailed from a line of chefs in her family. So what was up with the dinner? If he wasn't mistaken, he thought he'd smelled something similar to chili. He would soon find out.

"Tah-dah!" exclaimed Tamara proudly when Tyrell emerged from the restroom to the dinner table.

What the? he thought. I can't believe this! Oh my God, I'm dating myself!

Tamara had the paper plates stacked with the plastic utensils, paper napkins, tea lights, and a large plastic picture of Kool-Aid all decked out on the table. "Have a seat, sweetie, and I'll serve you your dinner," she offered.

Tyrell proverbially shook his head and merely seated himself at the table considerably edgy. Tamara surfaced with the turkey franks and bean dish in a microwave-safe container that was scorched somewhat, with slices of toast and a chilled wrapped half-stick of margarine. Damn, now that's cold! thought Tyrell.

Tyrell was tight-lipped during the meal. Tamara asked his opinion of it, and he nodded his head in contentment rather than lie to her face.

Tamara poured the Kool-Aid into their Styrofoam cups that washed down the meal that was especially dry from the scorched sauce.

After the meal, Tamara cleared the table by toting a garbage bag beside it and dumping everything into it including the ruined microwave dish. "Why don't you fetch the wine?" she requested.

"Sure," said Tyrell. He was dying to sneak peek into her refrigerator in the process of retrieving the wine.

"Well I'll be damned!" he cursed under his breath. Inside was a fully stocked fridge, including steaks, burgers, frozen dishes, luscious desserts, beer, eggs, milk, fruit, fresh veggies, and such. He retrieved the wine and covertly stormed into the room.

"What's the matter?" asked Tamara, noting his flustered expression.

"Nothing. I just stubbed my toe."

"I'm sorry." Tamara patted the couch and said, "Sit down beside me and let's have some wine. Be a dear and hand me those paper cups, would you?" Tyrell complied while staring LONGINGLY at the fully-stocked glass-door wine glass cabinet nearby.

The couple cuddled, drank wine, and watched television until late. And while Tyrell enjoyed this part of the evening the most, he was way past trying to get with Tamara at this point and dying to escape. He was hungrier than a mofo and had planned to stop at Rally's Burger Joint homeward bound.

The couple kissed goodnight and Tamara noticed Tyrell dashing to his car a tad faster than usual. She chuckled and closed the curtains.

Tamara headed up the back stairs to her two-bedroom apartment. She lived in a two-flat that was passed onto her by her late grandmother and the studio had been vacant indefinitely. She was using it to entertain guests until it was rented. Tyrell was none the wiser.

Tamara rather cocky and full of herself now, gloated aloud, "That'll teach him not to try to get over on me like that. You've got to stay on your toes and wine and dine me, if you want somma Tamara. Maybe you'll get lucky and maybe you won't; it's my prerogative," she concluded.

However, there was no mistaking; Tamara was definitely into Tyrell. He was a hard-working mechanic with convictions, not bad-looking in a

Nick Cannon sort of way, clean, so she imagined, and willing to go the distance in allowing a lady to show him how she desired to be treated and commit.

Tyrell was a keeper from what she'd seen of him so far. He'd passed the three-month rule test with flying colors. Now let us see how far we can go, she thought.

From here on in, Tamara resigned to relax her boundaries somewhat and allow things to take its natural course. But in the meantime, she was going to keep just-in-case booty-call Hunky Dexter and continue to see other people. And may the best man win!

Tyrell was kicking himself along the drive home. He'd spilled condiments all over his good shirt from his burger. He reflected on Tamara's refrigerator full of food and deliberated over why she'd served him slop instead of some of that good stuff she had.

Tyrell was animated, cussing, and swearing, calling Tamara a waste of time, and then caught himself. He had an epiphany. He surmised all this time she was fronting like she had it going on, when in fact, the only thing she had going was a decent job and car, so he imagined. That tiny place of hers was about the size of a thimble. And that ole outdated Magnavox TV; come on, who and the hell still had one of those?

Mulling it over further and delusional, Tyrell convinced himself she undoubtedly needed all that food in her fridge to stretch over a couple of paychecks. He relaxed his judgements about Tamara and decided he'd stick it out a tad longer and see what would happen next. Let's hope Mr. Tyrell Jr. can hold off a little while longer too, he thought, eying his crotch. Clearly, she needs a man to be with her and look after her, he thought. And he'd decided to endeavor to be that man.

Chapters 9

Henceforth the couple dated fervently and were setting off fireworks like gangbusters. The heat was so fierce between them they decided to take their relationship to another level. They beached it, attended movies, museums, concerts, and such. They fraternized with friends and family. Tyrell's family grew to love and embrace Tamara and her family him likewise.

Tyrell come hell or high water determined Tamara was a keeper, and sealed the relationship with a proposal and suggestion of a wedding date. He'd never met anyone like Tamara. She was full of encouragement and now ensured him she had his back. Even his momma liked her, which was a first. He was lovesick, alright.

Tamara capitulated wholeheartedly and fired Hunky Dexter, who resisted initially, but acquiesced, henceforth honoring her newfound commitment. She truly loved Tyrell and it was clear they were equally yoked. Everything was all set and good to go up to a point.

Tamara was hot as a firefly. She was ready to give Tyrell all of herself. She fancied herself as his wifey, which stuck in her mind like glue. She'd made romantic plans for their special evening tonight at her place, except there was just one itty-bitty catch.

Tyrell was ecstatic and beside himself with anticipation. He was doing the *'I'm gonna get me some,'* jig. He ransacked his closet for some fancy duds, made his decision, dressed, and even packed a stayover bag. Earlier he'd had a manicure and pedicure. He'd purchased wine and flowers. He hopped into his vehicle and headed to Tamara's, happy as two pigs in a blanket.

Tamara was waiting for Tyrell alright, in a revealing slinky red dress. She had a steak and potato dinner prepared, a formally set table, with a fancy center piece, her good wine glasses, cloth napkins, candles, an ice bucket, and all the trimmings. Home and Glamor Magazine had nothing on her.

Tyrell arrived promptly at seven. Tamara awarded him with a succulent kiss and tight squeeze, and lured him in with a red-manicured finger. She seized the wine and flowers after thanking him, and motioned him to the sofa. Tamara cozied up to him.

"You look and smell great, Babe.

"So do you. And your table is dope."

"Anything for my man," said Tamara, goo-goo-eyed.

ANYTHING?! thought Tyrell. Tamara in the doggie-style position panting in the heat of passion with him pumping her quickly came to mind.

The couple kissed passionately. It was getting hot and heavy. Tyrell's hand slithered up Tamara's dress like a vine. He was hoping to hit the Jackpot! BINGO! Wait! Panties? Why in the hell is she wearing those? Don't tell me she's going to fake me out! Oh no, not the curse! Tonight of all nights? Disillusioned, he withdrew his hand.

Tamara, oblivious to Tyrell's hysteria, rose and plucked him from the sofa. "Let's eat," she said, steering him toward the dinner table.

They both appeared to enjoy the meal, engaging in willy-nilly chit-chat. When Tamara was preoccupied, Tyrell alternated between disenchantment, marked by a curled lip, and sipping from his wine glass clueless about what to expect.

After the dishes were cleared, the couple returned to the sofa. Tamara studied Tyrell from the corner of her eye and discerned a bit of frustration. Perhaps she was mistaken, however, she'd given him the benefit of the doubt. Better safe and in love than sorry and in love, she thought. She'd made a decision and upheld it despite her reservations.

You see, earlier that same day, Tamara had run an errand. She'd garnered a set of papers and headed home. And despite a gazillion doubts and fears, she'd stuck to her guns and handled her business.

Tyrell was rather antsy on the sofa after dinner. He was ready to take the plunge. And just as he was about to tackle his fiancé, she ejected from the sofa.

"Dammit to hell!" he mumbled. "I was just about to dig in."

Next, he eyed Tamara riffling through her bag on her desk behind the sofa near the window. She returned to her seat with two sets of paperwork, set them on the cocktail table, and pulled out two pens.

Tyrell was outdone. What the?! he thought. I know this ain't what I think it is...oh *hell* no! Indeed, it was.

"Baby, please don't get offended, but I'm going to need you to fill these papers out. I have a set for me too. See? That way when the test results come back, we can share. Promise?"

Test results? Oh my freakin' God! Is this the Spanish Inquisition? Am I *ever* going to get any?!

SEXUALLY TRANSMITTED DISEASE QUESTIONNAIRE was posted across the top. There better be a pot of gold under that dress when I'm done with this. Jeez! thought Tyrell. Hhm, let me see here--name, address, phone, race-- I'mma put human. Let's see what else they're asking for.

Tamara momentarily sneak-peeked a few of Tyrell's answers over his shoulder and said, "You can't put that for race."

"Why? I already gave them my name, rank, and serial number. What more do they want—blood?"

Tamara stared at him blankly.

"You mean I gotta...?"

"Yup, and pee, too, babe. How else are they going to test us?"

"Strike what I said earlier; There better be ten pots of gold under that dress!" Tyrell muttered.

"What's that?" asked Tamara.

"Nothing. I was just thinking aloud."

Tyrell sized up the paperwork. The questionnaire appeared invasive and laborious to complete to him. Tyrell, frustrated to the max, had become quite belligerent.

Now, continuing on with the questionnaire, Tyrell began responding to the questions from top to bottom and thought to himself, let's see here: Nope, nope, nope, they really think I'mma answer this one with an honest answer? Good luck with that! For the next set of questions, he thought: Up yours! Kiss my... And these ones too? Asking me if what? Yeah, right!

Continuing on with the questionnaire -- Nope! Nope! None-yah! Nope! Bite me! Nope! Hecky naw! Eat this! Yo momma! he thought.

Unbeknownst to Tyrell, Tamara was studying him the entire time. She was leery of his defiant reaction to such probing questions gathered by his scathing expression.

And after much bastarding and moaning about the prying nature of the questionnaire, Tyrell finally completed it and returned it to his wifey-to-be. Tamara, quite pleased, squeezed Tyrell so tightly, he thought his insides would ooze out.

"No problem. You know I love you, gal!" So what's next, butt-naked, booty-slapping, hound dog sex—right?!" Tyrell blurted out jokingly.

"You bet!" said Tamara eyeing him coolly. Tyrell banging her doggie-style stark naked in cowboy boots and hat, howling, "Yah-hoo!" crossed her mind. She continued, "...that is after we return from the clinic and they take our blood and urine samples, the results come back negative, and we share them with each other as agreed. You're not worried are you?"

Tyrell cast Tamara a half-ass smile. "Do I look worried?" He was shakier than an earthquake inside.

Who does he think he's kidding? Tamara thought. He looks like he's about to blow!

Chapter 10

Over the next few days, following their clinic visit, the couple continued to engage over the phone. They were both nervous as two lobsters at a lobster fest while awaiting the test results.

When they both received the results and passed with flying colors, Tyrell was ecstatic. Alas he would have his pot of gold at the end of the rainbow or shall we say, up Tamara's dress.

Whew! I guess she's going to call me when she's ready. Nope, that's right. I dog, she cat. I chase the cat. Wait! Who made that mess up? Male dogs don't chase cats; they chase bitches! Well let's hope she's in heat because I'm ready to burn. I'm going to call her right now, thought Tyrell.

Tyrell phoned Tamara and the phone rang three times. Hhm, no answer. What's up with that? Okay, two more rings and I'm gone... Hhm, still no answer. Okay, two more...one, tw..."

"Hello?"

"Hey Babe.'"

"Who's this?"

"What?"

"Who are you?"

"It's me. You don't recognize my voice?!"

"Get lost, freak or I'mma call the cops!"

"Babe, it's me, Tyrell.

I know, fool!" Tamara in high spirits was giggling up a storm.

"Oh, Tamara's got jokes, eh?" Well, the joke's on you! I'm coming over! Bye!"

Tyrell was about to shower and thought, hell naw, she's got a shower. He packed an overnight bag and vamoosed to his vehicle.

Tamara was hot and excited. She'd been dying to make love to Tyrell. She fantasized about what type of lover he'd be. They'd only bumped and grinded short of intercourse.

He'd appeared a tad frantic. Contrarily, she preferred a man that took his time and paid attention to details. That's one of the things she adored about Tyrell though; that he appeared always amenable to moving at her pace and pleasing her.

On the drive to Tamara's, Tyrell was pensive and rambling. "I hope she doesn't think I'm going to be moving slow tonight. I'mma kiss it, flip it, slap it, lick it--whatever. I don't have time to play. I've got needs. And if she's serious about marrying me, she's got to put out and show me what I'm working with. I've waited long enough!" Tyrell proclaimed aloud.

"I've got the upstairs lit up and waiting for Tyrell. He's going to be shocked when he finds out about upstairs. The bed is all decked out with my gorgeous new bedding and 1000 thread count sheets and window treatments. He better hurry up!" Tamara proclaimed.

Tamara was the queen of bling-bling, mirrors, and animal prints combined with classic. Her space could be described as tribal-classic chic. This was also apparent in her fashion sense.

When Tyrell arrived, he nearly tackled Tamara to the floor. She giggled, then moaned, rubbing against his stiffness. So much for slow pace.

"Wait, Tyrell. Let me take you upstairs. I'm hot too, but I want our first time to be magical. Follow me."

Follow her? What the hell was she talking about? Is she holding back on me again? I swear I'll walk away from her for good if she's trying to blow me off! Oops, wrong choice of words, thought Tyrell. He dutifully followed Tamara upstairs with her pulling him along.

Tamara led Tyrell to her bedroom after a swift tour of her Glamor Home Magazine-like apartment.

"Dang!" he exclaimed. He cased her feng-shui-like space as she continued to lead him by the hand. They arrived to the bedroom and

Tyrell immediately tackled Tamara to the bed. They were excited about each other and in love. Tyrell abruptly stopped.

"Huh? What's the matter? Why'd you stop?" Tamara was really getting into it. She was hotter than a flatiron.

"Let's take a shower, babe. I didn't get a chance to before I came here."

"But I'm all dolled up and smelling fresh. I'll wait for you."

"Fat chance! Let's go, now!" Tyrell ordered. "You'll just have to repeat all that stuff again."

Tamara cheesed and followed Tyrell into the shower. The shower was a sensuous adventure. They explored every nook and cranny of each other thoroughly.

They returned to the bed, popped opened the wine, and partook of it. Intoxicated with the spirits and their love, they ravished each other throughout the wee small hours of the night.

At some point, the realization hit Tyrell that Tamara had hidden this part of herself from him, as he saw it, all whilst they were engaged. Why didn't he know about this space? What'd possessed her to hide it from him? What other secrets did she have? Was she born a man? Nah, he'd already confirmed that one. Then was she a criminal? A thief? A whore? He was livid to say the least.

Tyrell had laid all *his* cards and heart on the table whilst she was serving him a half deck. He had a good mind to seize his belongings and leave immediately. He judged himself to be a good man. So why didn't she trust him?

Tyrell was probing for answers. One thing for sure, he wasn't about to play into her hand and blow off all the good loving he had coming tonight. After all he'd gone through to get her? No way! Not on my watch, he thought. But tomorrow was another day. He'd show her!

Chapter 11

"You've got some interesting stuff in your cart. You must be a professional chef or caterer," remarked Barrett, a patron of the Ohio Gourmet and Spice Market.

"You caught that, huh?" responded Cee.

"Yes, I'm into catering myself. You ought to let me come to your place and bring you some samples."

"What? I don't know you like that."

"Hold up," said Barrett, "I'm sorry. I didn't mean any harm. I was just saying..."

"What?!" exclaimed Cee.

"Look, let's start over," said Barrett with his hands up. "My name is Barrett and you are...?"

"You can call me C, spelled C-e-e for caterer. How's that?"

"Hey, swell with me." Barrett ain't my real name either, he thought, tickled to pieces.

By the time they left the grocer, they were hitting it off. Barrett observed Cee pushing her cart to her car. Covertly, he studied her license plate, firmly planted it in his mind, and began trailing her home in an old rinky-dinky vehicle he'd borrowed from his roommate or stolen perhaps.

Barrett eventually having learned where Cee lived and who she really was, stood in the lurch studying her indefinitely. Over the next week he would track her every move, from the time she left her place, to her vehicle, to her job.

Barrett had a plan alright, and his victim was none the wiser. She'd misjudged his intentions to be honorable upon meeting him until she learned otherwise the hard way later down the road.

Up until and at the time Cee met Barrett, her boundaries were lax. She allowed men to set the pace for her despite her desire to move slowly. Barrett, a shyster and a trickster, was Mr. Romance to his victim, so she imagined, and he'd swept her off her feet. And as always the case, unsurprisingly he was a superb lover. He fit the predator profile to the T.

After a week of trailing his target and learning all Cee's moves, Barrett made it appear by happenstance that he was in the right place at the right time. "Hey, aren't you that lady from the store?" he asked, approaching Cee.

"Oh yeah, I remember you. Fancy meeting you again. Are you following me?" she asked, chuckling.

"Now why would I do that? Well, anyway, it seems we keep running into each other, so it must be in the stars for us to connect. I'd love to take you to dinner. Here's my card."

"Barrett's Catering Service, eh? You really *are* a caterer, huh?" said Cee, impressed, like anybody couldn't have gotten those cards printed. What was she thinking?

"I told you I was, so how about we hook up some time and exchange recipes?"

"Okay, I'll tell you what, I'll meet you somewhere, and if we hit it off, I'll give you my number. How's that?"

"Fair enough. How about Tommy's Diner on west Broad Street at seven?"

"Cool, that's not too far from my place. See you then, okay?"

"Sure," said Barrett serpentinely, and waving as Cee headed across the street.

Naturally, over dinner, Barrett adapted the customary idiosyncrasies of being the perfect gentleman and strumming Cee with compliments. He could charm the pants off his half-brother's sister's auntie's cousin's mother-in-law. The couple hit it off rather well to the point where Cee shortsightedly offered him her number.

Barrett was a swarthy, tall, well-groomed, and athletic-stunning-looking man. He masqueraded himself as chivalrous and scholarly. He courted Cee extensively after their initial rendezvous. He claimed his vehicle was in the shop so they cabbed it everywhere they went. He wined and dined her at swanky places. She'd become swept up in the romance of their relationship. And in only a whisper of time, they'd become lovers.

Cee never knew where he stayed; Barrett was quite elusive about it, claiming he bunked with friends and had little to no privacy at his place. You would think her antennas would've shot through the roof, however she'd become blinded by the sex by then. Having fallen for him so deeply and quickly, she'd lost all sense of herself and evolved around him.

After his second stayover at her apartment, Barrett made his move. He waited until Cee was in a deep sleep and stole away into the night with her vehicle. He'd secured a copy of her house and vehicle keys and slipped back to her home and bed surreptitiously.

Weeks afterwards, Barrett habitually slithered into the night when Cee was asleep during his stayovers, and would meet up with a woman named Portia. Their relationship was terse and abusive.

Presently, the moon spews its radiance upon the scantily leafed trees that swerve like hula dancers against the gentle breeze. Grafitied and boarded-up properties paint the backdrop. Refuse and contraband residue litter the walkways.

Barrett pulls up to the curbside in a stylish vehicle. He's come to fetch his sidekick, Portia.

"Where'd you get that fancy car from?" asks Portia, emaciated and edgy.

"Look, I told you not to question me, heifer. Just hop in and enjoy the ride," urges Barrett.

The denizens rabble-rouse around town like bandits. "Look, I gotta go!" says Barrett, hours later.

"Already? Where are you going so fast?" demands Portia.

Abruptly, a waft of persecutory cloud looms over Barrett prompting him to park curbside on Long Street. Portia's tone has knocked him out the box, somehow triggering memories of his womanizing abusive father and his mother's desertion.

Varicose-like vessels outline his neck. His eyes glaze over as he roars, "Didn't I warn you about questioning me?! Perhaps this'll serve as a reminder to you!"

Impassioned and crazed, Barrett viciously back-hands Portia into next week, disfiguring and bloodying her lip. Terror-stricken and remorseful, Portia cowers in her seat, swabbing her lip with the back of her hand, shielding her face and sniveling.

"Look, I'm sorry, okay? I got it now!"

"Good, then we have an understanding. Get out! See Yuh!"

Barrett speeds off abandoning Portia at the curbside, eyeing her through his rearview mirror and snickering. She'd been thrust into a ghost town of forsaken hopes and dreams mired in a crumbling wasteland of wreckage, boarded up buildings, and crack houses. Three would-be thugs eagle-eye her and storm in her direction...

The next morning, Cee traveled to work, none the wiser of Barrett's treachery. Departing work, she stepped outside, and after an avid search of her vehicle, determined it to be missing. Dumbfounded and distraught, she phoned the police. Come to find out, not only had Barrett stolen it, he'd secured a van using her credit cards and completely cleaned out her place.

Barrett had shrewdly selected the daytime knowing most of the community would be at work. No one witnessed anything, so they claimed, thus he'd gotten away clean.

Unsurprisingly, it turns out, everything Barrett said about himself was fraudulent. When Cee had visited the police station, her description matched that of a diabolical con artist who was a well-known predator of vulnerable women. It took her over two years and life coaching to reclaim her dignity, trust, and peace of mind, to restore her credit, and to obtain a brand new vehicle again.

Chapter 12

He'll call. I know he will. He's just angry right now. He'll get over it. Tamara was pacing her bedroom still in her nightie from last night. Like I said, he'll call... she thought, delusional after not hearing from Tyrell later on the next morning. I refuse to call him. Yeah, I'mma let him sweat a little. After all, I am his fiancé. And pretty soon, he'll be thirsty for somma Tamara. Yeah, that's how I'm going to play it, she thought.

By the end of the day, Tamara was waxing and waning in her bed staring at her cell phone nervously. Okay, okay, she reasoned. He's probably really busy right now. He'll call me perhaps tomorrow like he always does every night. DAY TWO: Same scenario—no phone call. DAY THREE: 8:00 a.m., 12:00 p.m., 4:00 p.m., 8:00 p.m.—no phone call.

At eight in the evening, Tamara, frustrated, decided to take a nap for a couple of hours. Her usual bedtime was around ten or so. The alarm clock sounded and she stretched. Remaining supine, she stared at her cell phone waiting for it to ring until her eyelids collapsed and she crashed.

Over a cup of coffee, the following morning, Tamara pondered what happened. What did I do? I thought things were cool between us three nights ago. Tyrell seemed pleased too. What changed? Is he getting cold feet? Was it the sex? Nah, I know better than that. My cooking? My...? Oh snap, she thought. And the realization hit her.

What was I thinking? I should've told him about upstairs months ago. He must feel betrayed about now. But he'll call—right?

Tamara reflected on Barrett. She thought she'd left all that baggage behind her. However, apparently she was still lugging it. She realized she should've explained about Barrett months ago and been more open and vulnerable with Tyrell.

Tyrell was rather easygoing and a decent listener, open and honest, as far as she could tell. And she truly believed he would've supported her had she only allowed him the chance to.

But *no*, she had to prove to him she was tough as nails and not one to toy with. After all, she had her pride and dignity--right? She had boundaries and believed in following the rules. But the problem is, she hadn't learned to be flexible or that rules were made to be broken or at the least, bent. And now that the realization had hit her, she wondered if it was too late.

Tamara thought the Barrett demons had been vanquished. But apparently they were still alive and kicking like gangbusters. She needed to nip this in the bud like yesterday. Cee needed to be laid to rest.

"I've already tried calling Tyrell and left several messages. I'm just going to have to be vulnerable now, put my big girl panties on, and explain and grovel for his forgiveness, that is if he'll still have me," Tamara muttered as she shed crocodile tears. Next, she dried her eyes as best she could and headed toward Tyrell's place, hopeful.

Tyrell lamented over Tamara. He missed her and desired to make love to her, but his pride overruled his heart. He was tempted to return her calls, but his anger had not subsided. He feared what he'd say or do. In his mind there was only a tiny crack of window to crawl through he'd left open for her to explain herself. It was only a matter of time.

Unbeknownst to Tamara, Tyrell had been down in the doldrums, sulking for two days in his bed and pajamas, watching television, and flicking mindlessly from channel to channel. He was depressed, delusional, and love-struck. He was praying something good would materialize soon.

Straightaway, the doorbell rang. Tyrell presumed it was Tamara! He was ecstatic! He had knots in his throat. He was edgy and suspicious. What the hell was she up to now? he thought.

Tyrell decided to stall to build up anticipation. I'll open the door in my boxers. She'll think I have female company. Serves her right! Wait! Will this work? Or will it backfire?!

Tyrell fraught with panic, followed his gut despite this. He lingered a bit; waited a minute more; the doorbell rang again; he paused again; one... two... three... Okay NOW! He peeked through the peep hole and flung open the door.

Tyrell caught Tamara in his arms as she fell into them wailing. The remainder of the fraganagle foolishness he was plotting flew out the door. He gingerly assisted her to the sofa where she further sobbed on his shoulder. She immediately broke down her story to him. He was understanding and sympathetic.

Chapter 13

The overhead lights shed a beam of bling-bling that illuminated the dining and dancing guests. A raised stage accommodated the band and DJ nearby. Laughter, music, and gaiety resounded in the air. The guests raised their glasses to toast the couple and cheered them on.

The courtyard was surrounded by lush jungle-like foliage with the sounds of a tranquil waterfall nearby thereby enhancing the splendor and romance of the ceremony. The landscape and overhead lights were warm and welcoming. Shortly before nightfall, the butterflies fluttered amongst the flowering shrubs and foliage presenting an enchanting glow and ambience.

Earlier, the guests were seated in rows divided by an isle carpeted with rose petals, who sighed and admired the ceremony between Tyrell and Tamara. It'd been an amazingly breathtaking balmy day and evening.

"I give you my heart and my eternal love and support," Tyrell pledged to Tamara, the couple standing beneath the Arbor and he lifting her veil. She displayed the ugly-face-cry joyful expression as she nodded her head in acceptance of his vows. She vowed to love him likewise; that'd she'd no longer withhold anything from him again in life. They both pledged their love to one another eternally.

"You are now man and wife," announced the minister. "You may kiss your bride."

A while back, Tyrell decided to pair off Ashley and Regina with Gunner and Luke, not out of spite, but hoping for a positive connection between them. After all, he figured Gunner and Luke, both drama

47

kings, would welcome the challenge. Ashley and Regina clinging to the arms of their dates, glared at each other as they strolled over to the reception area.

A year later, Tamara and Tyrell were yet hanging in there. They purchased a beautiful home together with the success they shared of their combined careers and Tyrell's burgeoning mechanic shop they and their friends and family together invested in. There was talk of a baby coming soon.

Chapter 14

The evening was brisk. The full moon cast its radiance throughout the large picture window. This particular Saturday eve, Tyrell and Tamara were anticipating a quiet evening with friends. Really?

Tyrell's buddies, Gunner and Luke appeared with dates, Ashley and Regina, to participate in this evening's soiree. The plan was to enjoy a nice dinner and afterwards catch a movie on the hosts' new 55-inch, HD, 3D flat screen, theater-style television with surround sound.

The doorbell chimed when Gunner and Luke appeared with their dates, Ashley and Regina. Tamara immediately steered them to the restroom to freshen up as she retrieved their outer garments. Ashley bedazzled by Tamara's home, commented.

"Your home is dope, Tamara."

"Why thank you, Ashley."

"It's all-ight," whispered Regina to Ashley when Tamara was out of earshot.

"You're just jealous," said Ashley. "This place looks like it came straight out of Home and Glamor Magazine, and you know it."

"Whatever!" said Regina flippantly, giving Ashley the hand and scrunching her nose with curled lip.

The men emerged from the restroom and the guests cozied up on the sectional sofa, sipping wine, nibbling hors d'oeuvres, and marveling at the spanking new television. Tamara indulged in a few appetizers momentarily then departed to assist her husband in the kitchen soon after which the couple appeared through the swinging door and announced dinner. They all piled into the rustic-safari-classic-style dining room. The rustic décor was a compromise and reflection of more of Tyrell's taste, replacing the bling-bling except in the place settings and napkin holders.

Ashley and Regina immediately flopped into seats tagged with their names on the place setting without as much as an afterthought. Gunner and Luke eagerly squatted between them oblivious to their lack of gallantry.

Tamara having peeped the entire scenario cringed at Ashley and Regina's haplessness of the situation and shook her head covertly. Thank God my baby was raised right 'cause Momma Tyrella don't play that, she thought.

The sixsome enjoyed a scrumptious meal of rack of lamb with mint glaze, baby carrots, peas, and pearl onions; asparagus wrapped in hollandaise sauce, jasmine rice, and apple pie alamode for dessert served with wine, tea, and coffee.

Afterwards, Tyrell offered to clear the dishes in lieu of his expectant wife doing so. He requested the assistance of his buddies who squawked in protest, but nonetheless acquiesced.

The women were paired off together in awkwardness having common knowledge of their relationship with Tyrell. However, they managed to make it to the sofa and engage in civilized chit-chat and sipping wine, with tea for Tamara.

Tyrell and his boys popped popcorn and organized the snacks supplied by Ashley and Regina. And the three headed through the swinging door to the living room. They all gathered before the massive television and watched a movie.

There was a discussion following the movie in the kitchen with coffee and snacks. Foolishly, Gunner and Luke raved about the beauty and booty of certain characters in the film of the female persuasion to the disapproval of Ashley and Regina who were utterly offended. What were they thinking?

An argument was instigated by Ashley and Regina, their dates besieged with a hodgepodge of neck-bowing and finger-pointing. Tyrell and Tamara outdone fled the scene.

"Hey, if you think she's so fly, why don't you get with her instead? I'm outta here!" cried Ashley, flying off the handle, finger-snapping and neck-bowing at Gunner, and preparing to bolt from the table.

"Girl, I'm right behind you. I'm not taking that mess either!" declared Regina.

Same ole, same ole.

The foursome continued quarreling amid Gunner and Luke protesting their dates leaving them. So rooted in their fraganagle psychodrama, they hadn't noticed Tyrell and Tamara's escape through the patio door.

Tyrell and Tamara lingered in the moonlight with Tamara's backside propped against Tyrell who gingerly massaged her pregnant belly. They smiled and groped each other momentarily. Intermittently they'd glance at the picture window showcasing the animated buffoonery of their guests.

"Those four were made for each other, weren't they?" asked Tamara, tickled.

"No doubt," replied Tyrell, chuckling.

Upon their last observation, it appeared the feud had finally ended. Tamara retreated into the house to check on the guests who'd appeared to call a truce. Tyrell lingered outside for his baby to inform him when the coast was clear. He abhorred drama. Really?

Meanwhile, a dark figure is lurking along the outer periphery of the backyard wrought-iron fence. He catches a glimpse of Tyrell and Tamara. "She should've been mine!" he scowls.

As he is glaring at Tyrell, passionate memories of Tamara dredge up deep-seated resentment of him. "I'll show him!" he gloats. Luck has it, Tamara left momentarily leaving the patio sliding door cracked open for her return. The scowling prowler is ecstatic and mumbles maniacally, "Good, here's my chance!"

He cranks his arm like a baseball picture preparing to pitch, coddling a medium-sized stone he'd retrieved along the fence in his palms. He aims it at Tyrell who is propped in front of the cracked-opened patio door awaiting Tamara's return. "Here goes nothin'!" utters Hunky Dexter, when abruptly Tamara pops through the sliding door as he hurls it.

The End

Afterword

Ladies, allow a man to show *you* how he feels about you. Show him how you feel about *yourself* by your standards. Date other people until he's ready or find someone else.

Guys, take it at her pace. If you man up and she warms up to you, she may come around. But don't expect her to have your back until you're fully committed and feel trustworthy and safe to her.

Be forewarned, sex for the most part can become an eternal connection. Hence, never take it for granted.

Finally, breached boundaries always signal unsafety and mistrust. However, boundaries should be relaxed as trust and commitment flows, because a closed door is never welcoming until it's opened.

Printed in the United States
By Bookmasters